STARTING OUT

I0894349

CREATIVE EDUCATION • CREATIVE PAPERBACKS

PUBLISHED BY CREATIVE EDUCATION AND CREATIVE PAPERBACKS
P.O. Box 227, Mankato, Minnesota 56002
Creative Education and Creative Paperbacks are imprints of The Creative Company
www.thecreativecompany.us

LIBRARY OF CONGRESS CATALOGING-IN-PUBLICATION DATA
Names: Riggs, Kate, author.
Title: Baby bears / Kate Riggs.
Series: Starting out.
Summary: A baby bear narrates the story of its life, describing how physical features, diet, habitat, and familial relationships play a role in its growth and development.

Identifiers: ISBN 978-1-64026-073-3 (hardcover)
ISBN 978-1-62832-661-1 (pbk)
ISBN 978-1-64000-189-3 (eBook)
This title has been submitted for CIP processing under LCCN 2018939104.

CCSS: RI.K.1, 2, 3, 4, 5, 6, 7; RI.1.1, 2, 3, 4, 5, 6, 7; RF.K.1, 3; RF.1.1

DESIGN AND PRODUCTION
by Chelsey Luther and Joe Kahnke
Art direction by Rita Marshall
Printed in the United States of America

PHOTOGRAPHS by Alamy (blickwinkel, F1online digitale Bildagentur GmbH, Lennette Newell), Can Stock Photo (Dreamframer), Getty Images (Mint Images/Art Wolfe), iStockphoto (vzmaze), Minden Pictures (Ingo Arndt/NPL, Klein and Hubert, L Lee Rue/FLPA), National Geographic Creative (Barret Hedges), Shutterstock (Bohbeh, Tony Campbell, critterbiz, Fascinadora, Rosa Jay, Jeff McGraw, David Rasmus, Egor Vlasov)

FIRST EDITION HC 9 8 7 6 5 4 3 2 1
FIRST EDITION PBK 9 8 7 6 5 4 3 2 1

baby BEARS

KATE RIGGS

CONT

ENTS

I AM A CUB.

I am a baby bear.

Look at my fluffy fur!

I was born in a den.
I weighed less than
one pound (0.5 kg).

My mother kept me safe and fed me food. It was winter then.

Now I love to
play and climb.
I wrestle with my
two siblings.

I investigate everything in springtime. What does this taste like?

My mother shows me what to eat.

We find grasses, roots, nuts, and berries. Ants and other insects are crunchy!

Eating food helps me grow.

I use my claws to dig in the dirt.

In the summer, we swim.

My legs are getting stronger. Soon I will be catching fish!

We look
for a den
in the fall.

We will stay warm
there the next winter.

I am
a young
bear now!

SPEAK AND LISTEN

OOWL!

Can you speak like a cub? Black bears moan, grunt, growl, and make other sounds. Listen to these sounds:

https://www.bear.org/website/bear-pages/black-bear/communication/29-vocalizations-a-body-language.html

Now it is your turn!

CUB WORDS

den: a small, hidden area where an animal rests

fur: the hair that covers some animals

insects: small animals with six legs and usually one or two pairs of wings

investigate: to study in order to find out more about something

siblings: brothers or sisters